More
Five-Minute
Devotions
for Children

CELEBRATING GOD'S WORLD AS A FAMILY

Written by Pamela Kennedy and Douglas Kennedy
Illustrated by Amy Wummer

ideals children's books.
Nashville, Tennessee

ISBN-13: 978-0-8249-5502-1
ISBN-10: 0-8249-5502-1
Published by Ideals Children's Books
An imprint of Ideals Publications
A Guideposts Company
Nashville, Tennessee
www.idealsbooks.com

Color separations by Precision Color Graphics, Franklin, Wisconsin

Printed and bound in Italy by LEGO

Library of Congress Cataloging-in-Publication Data

Kennedy, Pamela, date.
  More five-minute devotions for children : celebrating God's world as a family / written by
Pamela Kennedy and Douglas Kennedy ; illustrated by Amy Wummer.
     p. cm.
  ISBN-13: 978-0-8249-5502-1
  ISBN-10: 0-8249-5502-1 (alk. paper)
  1. Children—Prayer-books and devotions—English. I. Kennedy, Douglas, date. II. Wummer,
Amy. III. Title.
  BV265.K46 2004
  242'.62—dc22

                                                            2004015525

Lego_Jun10_2

Designed by Eve DeGrie

Scripture quotations are taken from the *Holy Bible,* New Living Translation, copyright © 1996.
Used by permission of Tyndale House Publishers, Inc., Wheaton, Illinois 60189. All rights
reserved.

For Mom, who always remembered to love. –P.J.K.
For Lauren, who believes in me. –D.M.K.

In memory of our much-loved pets: Isaac, Pinchy, Hess,
Mobil, Jeff, Snoopy, Bibi, Bean, and Bart. –A.W.

Contents

Three-Toed Patience

Three-toed sloths live in the rain forest and spend their entire lives climbing around in trees. They take their time, patiently searching for just the right leaves to eat. In fact, sloths move so slowly that tiny plants called algae grow in their fur. After a long time, the algae turns their fur coats green. Slow-moving sloths use their green coats to blend in with the trees and hide from their enemies. It's hard for hunters like jaguars and eagles to find a little, green sloth in a big, green forest. Because sloths are slow and patient, they become almost invisible in the trees, safe from all the dangers around.

It is not always easy to be patient. Sometimes we do not want to wait for things. We want them right now. But getting things right now may not be best for us. Being patient with God means waiting for him to show us the best time for things. Sometimes it can be very hard to wait, but God promises us that if we are patient, he will help us grow in ways that are safe. God knows just the right time for everything.

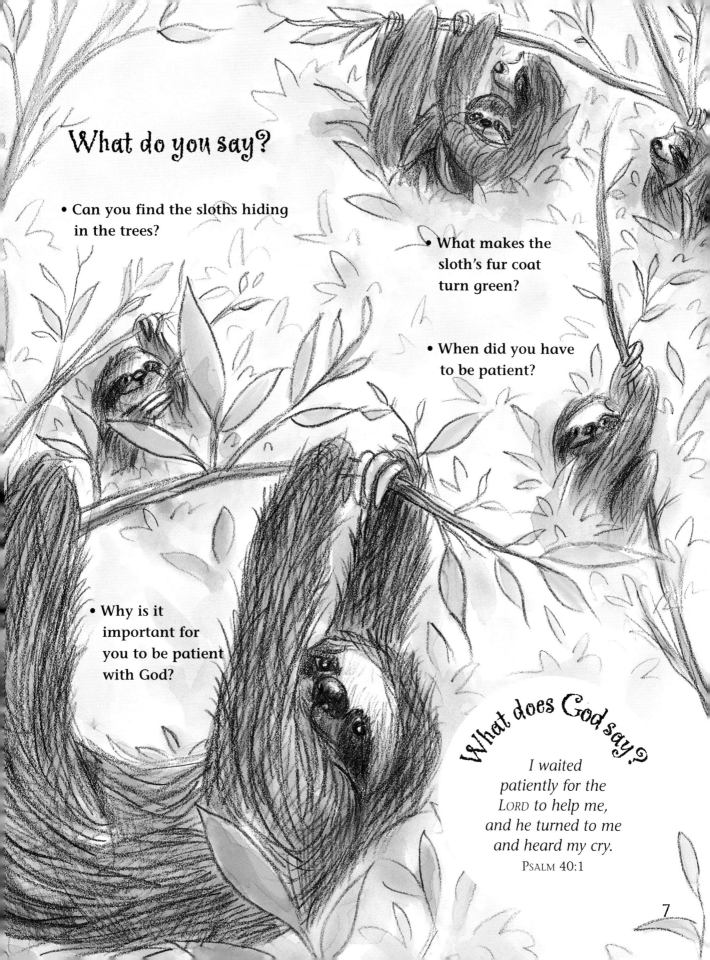

What do you say?

- Can you find the sloths hiding in the trees?

- What makes the sloth's fur coat turn green?

- When did you have to be patient?

- Why is it important for you to be patient with God?

What does God say?

I waited patiently for the LORD to help me, and he turned to me and heard my cry.

PSALM 40:1

7

Safety Stripes

Zebras look like horses with beautiful black and white stripes. Their stripes are pretty, but they are also important for the zebras' safety. When zebras are traveling across the open plains of Africa, it can be very dangerous. Lions wait to pounce on one that is slow or sick. So sometimes hundreds of zebras come together to travel in one giant herd! When lots of zebras get close to each other, all their stripes seem to blend together. This confuses the lions. It is hard for them to pick out one zebra to chase. The zebras know that if they stick together, they will all be safe from the lions.

We can learn a lesson from these beautiful, striped animals. There are times when it is difficult for us to be all by ourselves too. God knows that we are happier and safer when we learn to work together. This is called teamwork, or cooperation. When we cooperate with one another, we can have lots of fun. We can play games, act out stories, solve problems, and even help each other. The hard things seem easier when we can share them with others. It pleases God to see us work together. Because he made us, he knows we do our best when we learn to use teamwork.

What do you say?

- Can you count all the zebras in the picture?

- What happens when hundreds of zebras work together?

- What are some things you like to do with your friends?

- Why is teamwork important to God?

What does God say?

Then make me truly happy by agreeing wholeheartedly with each other, loving one another, and working together with one heart and purpose.
PHILIPPIANS 2:2

Fishy Neighbors

The cleaner wrasse is a tiny fish with some pretty big friends. Cleaner wrasses live on coral reefs and are sometimes known as "doctor fish" because they are so helpful to their neighbors. Every morning, the cleaner wrasse swims to an open spot on the reef. He does a dance to let the other fish in the area know that he is "open for business." All the larger fish that need to be cleaned that day form a line and patiently wait their turn. One by one, the big fish hold still while the cleaner wrasse cleans the bugs and dead skin off of their bodies. Sometimes, the cleaner wrasse even swims into the mouths of the big fish to clean their teeth!

A cleaner wrasse has to be pretty brave to clean his customers' teeth, especially when his customer is a shark or an eel. But these little fish don't get eaten because sharks and eels know that cleaner wrasses are helpers, not lunch. God wants us to be friendly with our neighbors and to lend them a hand when they need it. Good neighbors come in all shapes, sizes, and colors. It pleases God when we are helpful to all our neighbors.

What do you say?

- Who is being helped by the cleaner wrasses?

- Why are cleaner wrasses sometimes called "doctor fish"?

- Who do you know who could use your help?

- How has God helped you?

What does God say?

For the whole law can be summed up in this one command: "Love your neighbor as yourself."
GALATIANS 5:14

11

Trusty Pigeons

Pigeons are no strangers to the city. They fly from the roofs of tall buildings to the benches in parks, looking for bread crumbs and other small bits of food. But some pigeons are highly trained delivery birds. Pigeons can be trained to carry tiny notes in metal bracelets across long distances. They have a very special ability to find their way around without getting lost. People who want to train pigeons to carry messages must first set their pigeons free and hope that the birds will come back.

It takes a lot of trust for a person to set their birds free. After all, it would be very easy for a pigeon to fly away and find a new home. But pigeons are trustworthy. God taught them to always come back to their real home, so a bird trainer can trust his pigeons to return. God wants us to be trustworthy too. Sometimes when we promise to do one thing, we actually feel like doing something else. God wants us to keep our promises; he wants us to be trustworthy. When we keep our promises it makes us more like him, because God is faithful and we can always trust him.

What do you say?

- Which pigeon is carrying a message?

- Why does a bird trainer have to trust his pigeons?

- What is a promise you have made? Are you keeping it?

- Why does God want you to be trustworthy?

What does God say?

Commit everything you do to the LORD. Trust him, and he will help you.
PSALM 37:5

Dogs on the Job

Dogs enjoy playing and running, digging in the snow, or catching a Frisbee on a summer afternoon. But did you know that some dogs also have jobs? There are dogs that have been trained to help people who cannot see. They keep their owners safe by guiding them around dangerous objects or helping them cross a busy street. Other dogs help people who cannot hear. They let their owners know when the phone is ringing or when a baby is crying and needs help. Some dogs work in airports to sniff for things that should not be taken on planes. Other dogs hunt for people who are lost in the snow or in dark places where people cannot see. When these dogs are working, they know it is important to stay on the job. When they are finished working, then it's time to play.

Just like dogs, children love to run and play too. But God tells us that we also have work or chores we need to do. Some children help their parents by cleaning up after meal times. Other children help take care of their younger brothers and sisters. Taking out the trash, folding clothes, and picking up toys are other chores children can do. In every family there is work that needs to be done. God wants us to work hard and to do our jobs without complaining. When the work is done, then everyone has time to play!

What do you say?

- Are the dogs in the picture working or playing?

- What kinds of work can dogs do?

- What are some chores you do at your home?

- Why do you think God wants us to do our work without complaining?

What does God say?

Commit your work to the LORD, and then your plans will succeed.

PROVERBS 16:3

Fleecy Fighters

Sometimes animals just can't get along. Bighorn sheep live high in the mountains and are not very friendly at all. Male bighorn sheep are called rams, and every autumn they get angry and fight. They run toward each other and slam their heads together. None of them wants to share territory with any of the other rams, so they fight to see which ones are the strongest. The strongest rams with the biggest horns can stay, but the weak rams with small horns have to find someplace new to live. A fight between two rams can last an entire day, and sometimes the fight only ends when the stronger ram kills the weaker one!

Some people like to fight, just like rams. Sometimes, people who are big and strong think they can get what they want by hurting smaller people. It is hard to be friends with someone like that. People who use words to settle their problems make much better friends than people who use their size. God would rather see us talk about our problems. When we are peaceful and friendly, we understand each other better—and we understand God better too!

What do you say?

- Which ram has the biggest horns?

- Why do rams slam their heads together?

- What makes you want to act like an angry ram?

- Why does God want us to talk about our problems instead of fighting?

What does God say?

Stop your anger!
Turn from your rage!
Do not envy others—it
only leads to harm.
PSALM 37:8

17

Smart Pigs

Lots of people think pigs are messy, smelly, lazy, and stupid. But people who really know pigs, like farmers and veterinarians, can tell us a different story. They know that pigs like being clean and that clean pigs don't stink. Pigs are also very active animals, and some people even train their pigs to run at special pig racetracks. But the most surprising thing about pigs is how smart they are. Animal experts agree that pigs are some of the smartest animals in the world. They learn quickly, and they can be trained to do all kinds of things. That's why so many people think pigs make wonderful house pets!

Even though pigs are clean, smart, and friendly, people tell stories that make pigs seem lazy and stupid. It isn't fair to pigs when people say mean things about them—especially because those things aren't true. Sometimes people like to judge others and say mean things about them, even when it's not true. God doesn't want us to waste our time judging others, and he doesn't like it when we say mean things that aren't true. He wants us to accept each other and be kind.

What do you say?

• What kinds of things are these pigs doing?

• What are some untrue things people have said about pigs?

• Have you ever said untrue things about someone else?

• Why doesn't God want us to judge others?

What does God say?

Stop judging others, and you will not be judged. Stop criticizing others, or it will all come back on you. If you forgive others, you will be forgiven.

LUKE 6:37

19

Happy Hummingbirds

Hummingbirds whiz around a garden like bumblebees. They are very tiny—five of them could fit in a person's hand! They have long, thin beaks with sharp tips, and when they fly, their wings move so fast they look like a blur! God planned every part of the hummingbird for a purpose. He made them tiny so they could fit inside flowers. He made their beaks long and thin so they could reach into blossoms and drink their nectar. He gave them speedy, little wings so they could zip from flower to flower. God made hummingbirds that way because he knew what they would need to be happy and healthy.

God knows what we need too. He gave us eyes so we can see beautiful colors and the faces of family. He gave us ears so we can hear music and the voices of our friends. He gave us minds so we can think and wonder and dream, and he gave us mouths so we can speak and sing. God knew just what we would need to be happy, healthy people. That's why he made each part of our bodies according to his wonderful plan.

What do you say?

- What are these hummingbirds doing?

- What do hummingbirds need?

- Can you think of five good ways you can use your hands?

- Why do you think God made you the way he did?

What does God say?

As we know Jesus better, his divine power gives us everything we need for living a godly life.
2 PETER 1:3A

21

Wild Horses

In jumping contests, trained horses leap over fences. In rodeos, horses help cowboys rope calves. All these horses began as babies, or foals, that had to be trained. Horses do not naturally allow people to ride on their backs. But when horses have been trained, they can accomplish many different things like pulling carts, running in races, or working on ranches. Without training, a horse may be wild and beautiful, but it cannot help anyone.

Just like horses, we all need to learn to do certain things. We do not naturally know how to be polite, to say "please" and "thank you," to pick up after ourselves, or to help others. Our parents and teachers must train us to do these things or we cannot be helpful to ourselves or to others. God knows that it is important for each of us to learn and grow. He knows we need people to help train us. But we need to be willing to learn and grow too. When we are willing to follow the directions our parents and teachers give us, we become better helpers.

What do you say?

- Can you find the foal in the picture?

- Why do horses need to be trained?

- What are some things your parents are teaching you to do?

- Why do you think God wants you to obey your parents and teachers?

What does God say?

Children, obey your parents because you belong to the Lord, for this is the right thing to do.
EPHESIANS 6:1

23

Bossy Donkeys

Male donkeys are called jacks. These animals do not make very good pets. They don't like to be ridden. They often bite and chase other animals and sometimes will even stomp on a smaller animal that wanders into their corral. Jacks also like to bray or make a loud noise that sounds like *ah-ee, ah-ee, ah-ee*! They often have to be separated from the other donkeys because they cannot seem to get along.

Some people may act like jack donkeys. Sometimes they just can't get along with others. They hit or yell or chase other people. They want to tell everyone else what to do, and they do not listen when others have something to say. Bossy people, just like bossy donkeys, may end up all alone. Others find it hard to play with them. God wants us to have friends and to be a good friend. Good friends listen to one another and share their toys. They do not hit or yell at each other. When we are kind and share with our friends, they like playing with us. It pleases God when good friends get along.

What do you say?

- Which of the donkeys in the picture is braying?

- Why don't jack donkeys make good pets?

- What are some things you can do to be a good friend?

- Why do you think it makes God happy when friends get along?

What does God say?

A friend is always loyal.
PROVERBS 17:17A

Little Ladybugs

Ladybugs like to crawl on leaves and sometimes on people's arms. They are small members of the beetle family, usually less than a quarter of an inch long. They come in lots of colors from red to brown to black, and many of them have small spots on their *elytra*, or wing covers. Ladybugs are a gardener's friend because they eat the small insects that destroy plants. But ladybugs have some strange ways of doing things. They don't have noses, but they smell with their feet! And they do have mouths, but they taste things with their two antennae! The ladybug's way of doing things is different from ours, but she gets along very well.

People like to do things differently too. Not everyone likes the same things or does things in the same way. Sometimes when people do things differently from us, we think they are wrong. We think our way is the right way. But God reminds us that we should enjoy our differences and not criticize others. Sometimes it's fun to try to do things in a new or different way. We might learn something we didn't know before.

What do you say?

- Can you count all the ladybugs in the picture?

- How does a ladybug smell and taste things?

- What are some things you do differently from your friends?

- Why do you think God wants us to enjoy our differences?

What does God say?

Show respect for everyone. Love your Christian brothers and sisters.
1 PETER 2:17A

Cuddly Kittens

When kittens are born, they are very small. Their little eyes aren't even open until a week or two later. They cannot walk well and they need their mothers to take very good care of them so they will be safe. They can be hurt easily if they are not held carefully, or if they are squeezed too tightly. Kittens need to stay warm too. If they get too cold, they could die. But if a kitten is well cared for by its mother, and if it is protected while it is still very young, it will grow up to be a healthy, happy cat.

It is good to be gentle and to protect baby animals from harm, to treat them with kindness and to care for them. But sometimes people need special care too. There are times when we all feel weak or small. We might be frightened or just not very strong in some way. That's when we need family and friends to help and protect us. God knows that we are all weak at times and he wants us to show gentleness and love to one another. He wants us to help and care for each other so we can all grow up to be healthy and happy people.

What do you say?

- What are these kittens doing?

- Why do you think God wants you to be a kind and gentle friend?

- Why do kittens need to be protected?

- When have you felt like you needed someone to protect and care for you?

What does God say?

Gentle words bring life and health.
PROVERBS 15:4A

Unseen Heroes

Many people think that earthworms are yucky and boring. They do not think of these creatures as heroes in the animal kingdom. They only see them wriggle around in the dirt. But these people don't know the whole story. Without worms, the earth would not be able to produce healthy fruits, vegetables, flowers, and trees. All day long, every day, earthworms are like underground farmers. They make holes in the dirt so that air can get into the soil. This is called aerating. They also enrich the soil with their waste products, called castings. Good soil can have as many as one million worms in an acre! Those million worms can eat ten tons of leaves, stems, dead bugs, and dead roots in a year.

Just because we can't see the worms doing their work, doesn't mean they aren't important. Without them, the world would not be as healthy or beautiful. Sometimes people are like that too. Many people do quiet things that are very important. Others may not see what they do, but God sees all the good things and he knows who the real heroes are. We might worry that we are doing good things but no one seems to notice. God knows what we are doing and will bless us for being unseen heroes.

What do you say?

- Where are all the earthworms in the picture?

- What are some of the good things worms do?

- What are some good things you have done that no one knows about?

- Why do you think God blesses unseen heroes?

What does God say?

Give your gifts in secret, and your Father, who knows all secrets, will reward you.

MATTHEW 6:4

31

Helpful Honkers

Geese like to fly in groups across the sky, making their honking sound. When geese travel, they fly together in a *V* formation. There is an interesting reason why they do this. When they fly in a *V*, each goose gets an extra boost from the goose ahead of it. Because of the updrafts created by their flapping wings, the geese can fly much farther together than any one of them could alone. And the honking they do has a purpose too. The geese in the back of the *V* honk to encourage the ones up ahead to keep going. They cheer each other on! When the lead goose gets tired, he will move back and another goose will take his place. By taking turns in the lead, no one goose gets too tired and everyone gets a chance to be the leader.

Geese do many things to help and encourage one another. That's how God made them. People can do many things to help one another too, but sometimes we don't. Some people like to be first all the time. They don't enjoy cheering for others, and they may not even like helping others. These kinds of people could learn a lesson from geese. God is happy when we are kind to one another, helping and encouraging each other.

What do you say?

- How many geese are in the formation in the picture?

- Why do geese fly in a V formation?

- Who is someone you could encourage or help?

- Why do you think God might like you to learn a lesson from the geese?

What does God say?

Rejoice. Change your ways. Encourage each other. Live in harmony and peace. Then the God of love and peace will be with you.

2 CORINTHIANS 13:11B

33

Cheerful Chirpers

Crickets like to chirp at night in the fields. Sometimes, they get into people's houses and sing all night long! Crickets are small green or brownish insects about one inch long. Their name comes from a French word, *criquer*, that means "little creaker." Crickets make their chirping sound by rubbing their wings together. If they are frightened, they will stop and be very quiet. But if they feel safe, they are happy and they will continue making their cheery sound. A cricket's chirp can tell us how hot or cold it is. We can count the number of times a cricket chirps in fifteen seconds and add forty to that number to find out the temperature.

God created the cricket with a special way to make a cheerful sound. God has given us a way to make a cheerful sound too. We can sing together and share with others how happy we are. We can make up our own songs or sing songs that other people have written. Music is a way we can express our feelings, whether we are happy or sad. God tells us in the Bible that singing is a wonderful way to show that we love him.

What do you say?

- Which cricket in the picture is chirping?

- How can you tell the temperature by listening to a cricket's chirp?

- What is your favorite song? Can you sing it?

- Why do you think God loves to hear us sing?

What does God say?

Worship the LORD with gladness. Come before him, singing with joy.
PSALM 100:2

35

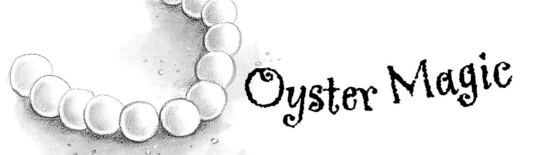

Oyster Magic

The oyster is a shellfish that lives in salt water. It doesn't make a sound or move or even look very pretty. But oysters create something that is very valuable. Oysters make beautiful, gleaming pearls. When a tiny grain of sand gets inside the oyster's shell, this grain of sand makes the oyster very uncomfortable. In response to this irritation, the oyster begins coating the grain of sand with something called *nacre*, made of protein and calcium. Layer after layer of nacre coats the grain of sand until, at last, a beautiful pearl is formed. Because of its pain the oyster creates something precious.

Sometimes things happen in our lives that seem sad or bad like the grain of sand feels to the oyster. Things make us irritated or unhappy. But God says that if we will trust him, he can bring good things out of the bad things that happen to us. He promises to never leave us. We can tell him about the bad or sad things and ask him to help us grow and learn from them. Then we can see God make something beautiful in our lives too.

What do you say?

- Can you find the pearls in the oysters?

- How does an oyster make a pearl?

- What's something sad or bad that has happened to you?

- How do you think God might bring something good from the sad or bad thing in your life?

What does God say?

And we know that God causes everything to work together for the good of those who love God and are called according to his purpose for them.

ROMANS 8:28

Monarch Miracle

Have you ever wondered where the beautiful orange and black monarch butterfly comes from? At the very beginning of its life, the butterfly is just a tiny white egg. When the egg hatches, a larva comes out. The larva eats and grows until it is a large, striped caterpillar. The caterpillar attaches itself to a twig and becomes very still. A hard, green covering grows over its body. This is called a pupa, or chrysalis. Inside, the caterpillar is quietly changing. In just a few weeks, the green shell cracks open and a beautiful black and orange butterfly climbs out. It stretches its wings in the sun and then it flies away.

Who could imagine that a big, striped caterpillar would ever become a graceful butterfly? Just like the caterpillar, we are becoming what God wants us to be. Sometimes it's hard to wait to grow up, but we can trust that God will help us every day. He promises he will always be with us and he tells us how to live in the Bible. When we believe him and do what he says, he helps us grow and change in all the right ways.

What do you say?

- Can you find the egg, the caterpillar, the chrysalis, and the butterfly?

- What comes out of a chrysalis?

- What do you think you would like to be when you grow up?

- Why is it a good idea to follow God's ways?

What does God say?

"For I know the plans I have for you," says the LORD. *"They are plans for good and not disaster, to give you a future and a hope."*
JEREMIAH 29:11

Hard-Working Turtles

Once a baby sea turtle hatches from its egg, it has to start on a very long journey. Mother sea turtles lay their eggs in the sand at the beach. When the eggs hatch, baby turtles pop out of the sand and inch their way back to the ocean. The trip to the sea is very hard since sea turtles don't have legs or feet—they only have little fins. For a brand new baby turtle marching across the beach on little fins, the smallest pile of sand seems like a giant mountain. And imagine what a crashing wave looks like to a newborn turtle the size of a person's thumb!

Once a new turtle makes it into the ocean, it has to swim for days to find a peaceful patch of kelp where it can rest and grow strong—and that's if it doesn't get eaten along the way. God knows being a baby turtle is hard. If a turtle works hard and doesn't give up, it can grow up to live in a peaceful cove, snacking on seaweed and jellyfish. God knows that being a person can be hard too, but we have to keep working hard and have faith that God wants us to succeed. God will never give up on us, and he doesn't want us to give up either.

What do you say?

- How many sea turtles are running to the sea?

- Why is it hard for a baby turtle to make it to the ocean?

- Have you ever felt like giving up?

- Why does God want us to work our hardest?

What does God say?

We are pressed on every side by troubles, but we are not crushed and broken. We are perplexed, but we don't give up and quit.

2 CORINTHIANS 4:8

Masked Meerkats

The markings on meerkats make them look like bandits. They look like little thieves because they have black stripes across their faces that look like masks. However, meerkats are not selfish like thieves; in fact, they're very friendly and helpful. Meerkats live in groups, called bands, with as many as forty members. Everyone in the band helps everyone else stay safe and get food. When a mother meerkat needs to go out and get food, other meerkats take turns babysitting the youngsters, even if it means missing lunch. When all the meerkats are out searching for food, one meerkat will climb a nearby tree to watch for danger. If it sees a hawk or a snake, it will call out to its friends below so they can run for safety. Meerkats also take care of each other by cleaning one another's fur. Meerkats are great helpers. They love to make sure everybody in the whole band is healthy and happy.

God likes to see meerkats being such wonderful helpers. Imagine how hard it would be for a mother meerkat to feed herself and her babies if all the other meerkats were selfish and she couldn't get a babysitter! God gives us lots of chances to be helpers, too. It pleases him when we aren't selfish and help the people around us.

What do you say?

- Which meerkats are helping others?

- How do meerkats help the others in their band?

- What is the difference between being selfish and being a helper?

- Why do you think God wants you to be a helper?

What does God say?

Don't be selfish. . . . Be humble, thinking of others as better than yourself.
PHILIPPIANS 2:3

Strange Creatures

A platypus is a very unusual critter. The only place on the planet where we can find this weird animal is in the creeks and swamps of eastern Australia. Platypuses have a bill like a duck but no feathers. Instead, they have fur like a cat. They have webbed feet like a seagull and a flat tail like a beaver. When they're upset, they can growl like a dog or strike out with their poison-tipped spurs. A platypus doesn't give birth like other furry animals—it lays eggs! It's safe to say that there is no other animal on earth like a platypus. In fact, when an explorer brought the first platypus to England, the people laughed at it. They said it wasn't even a real animal!

Sometimes we laugh at people who don't look like us. We make fun of them if they do things in ways that seem strange to us. This hurts their feelings and makes God sad too. God says he is the Father of all people. He has made each person. He knows where we will live and what we will look like. We should never try to make someone feel bad just because they don't look or act like us. God enjoys variety and every person is a part of God's wonderful creation. He loves each of us equally.

44

What do you say?

- What is the platypus doing?

- What are some things that seem strange about the platypus?

- Has anyone ever hurt your feelings?

- Why do you think God wants us to try to understand others?

What does God say?

And yet, LORD, you are our Father. . . . We are all formed by your hand.
ISAIAH 64:8

45

Dancing Cranes

For a long time, scientists couldn't figure out what whooping cranes were doing. Every year, during their migration, the tall, skinny birds land and begin hopping up and down, flapping their wings, and twirling around. Sometimes a flock makes a large circle, and all the birds strut and wiggle together in formation. But why, in the middle of a thousand-mile migration, would whooping cranes take time out to act so funny?

It turns out whooping cranes just like to dance! They fly and fly and fly—and that's hard work—but they take time to relax and have fun too. Some people could take a lesson from whooping cranes. They work so hard that they forget to play. God made the whole wide world for us. He wants us to work hard, but he also likes to see us enjoy ourselves. When we take time to play and have fun, we're celebrating what God has given to us.

What do you say?

- How many dancing cranes do you see?

- Why do whooping cranes stop in the middle of their migrations?

- Did you remember to play today?

- Why does God like to see us play?

What does God say?

Always be joyful.
I THESSALONIANS 5:16

Pamela Kennedy writes books for all ages of children. When not at the computer, Pam teaches part-time at a high school for girls and speaks at Christian retreats and conferences. She lives in Honolulu with her husband and their crooked-tailed cat. *More Five-Minute Devotions* is the first book that Pam co-wrote with her son, **Douglas Kennedy**. Doug lives in Seattle, Washington, where he writes for an interior design magazine. This is his first book.

Amy Wummer has been illustrating children's books for ten years. Her playful watercolor illustrations for *More Five-Minute Devotions* evoke the wonder of a child's delight in the world. She lives in Pennsylvania with her husband, also an artist, and their three children.